Jim and Jane and the Baseball Game

Written by Susannah Reed

Illustrated by Chloe Evans

Collins

Who and what is in this story?

Listen and say 1

cinema

Download the audio at www.collins.co.uk/839706

Mark
Jane
Julia
Mike
Jim

Bill
Bouncer

One day, Jim went to his friend Jane's house. He had a poster in his hand.

"Look at this," said Jim. "There's a baseball game on Saturday."

“I want to go,” said Jim. “Bill Bradley is my favourite player.”

“I like him, too,” said Jane. “Let’s ask my parents!”

Jane and Jim went into the living room.

“Mum,” said Jane. “Can I go to the baseball game on Saturday, please?”

“OK,” said Jane’s mum, “Let’s buy some tickets.”

Jane's mum looked on her computer.

"I'm sorry," she said. "There are no tickets for Saturday."

Then Jane had an idea.

"I know," she said. "Let's play baseball with our friends."

"Good idea," said Jim. "We can ask Mike and Julia. They love baseball."

“Can I go to the park?” asked Jane.

“Yes, you can,” said Jane’s dad.
“Go with Mark.”

Mark was Jane’s older brother. He loved baseball, too.

The baseball game was fun. Jane threw the ball to Jim. Jim hit the ball with his baseball bat.

"Wow," said Mark. "That was fantastic!"

But Jim said, “Oh, no! Look at that dog.
It’s taking the ball.”

The big dog caught the ball and ran into the playground. The children ran after it.

"Bad dog," said Mark. "Give the ball to me."

"Don't be angry," said Jane. "Look! It's only young, and it's afraid."

Jane looked at the dog's collar.

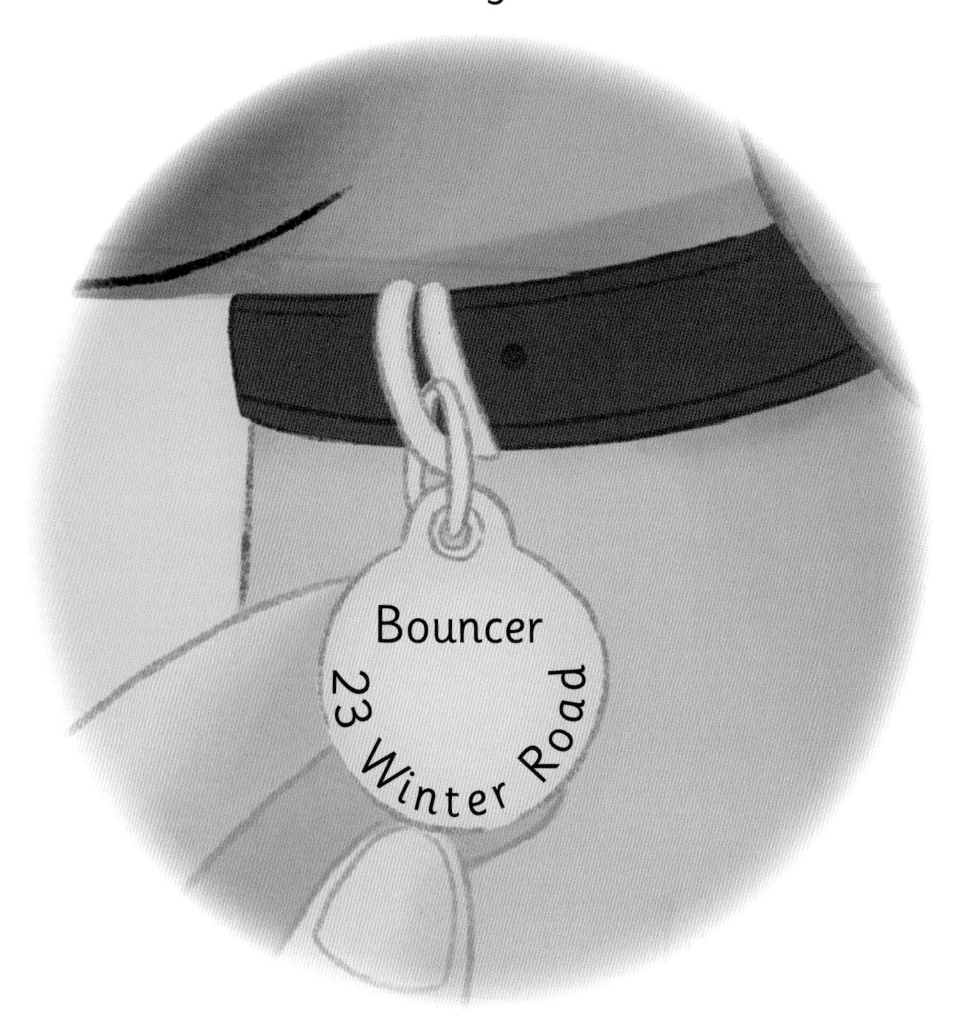

"His name is Bouncer!" she said. "And he lives at number 23, Winter Road."

"Where is that?" asked Jim.

“I know,” said Mark. “Winter Road is in the town centre.”

“Oh yes,” said Jane. “It’s next to the cinema.”

“Let’s take Bouncer home,” said Jim.

The children took Bouncer to Winter Road. They found number 23.

"Is this the right house?" asked Jim.

"Yes," said Jane. "Look!"

A man opened the door.

"Bouncer!" he said. "There you are!"

The children looked at the man.

"You're Bill Bradley!" said Jane.

“Yes, I am,” the man said, “And this is my dog Bouncer.”

“He was in the park,” said Jim. “He caught our baseball.”

“Bouncer loves baseball!” said Bill Bradley. The children laughed.

"Thank you for finding Bouncer," said Bill Bradley. "Would you like these tickets for a baseball game? It's on Saturday."

"Yes, please!" said the children. "Thank you!"

The children ran back to Jane's house.

"Mum and Dad," said Jane, "Can Jim and I go to the baseball game on Saturday? We've got some tickets!"

“Wow!” said Jane’s mum, “Yes, you can!”

“Can we come, too?” asked Jane’s dad.

“Yes,” said Jane, “We can all go!”

Picture dictionary

Listen and repeat 

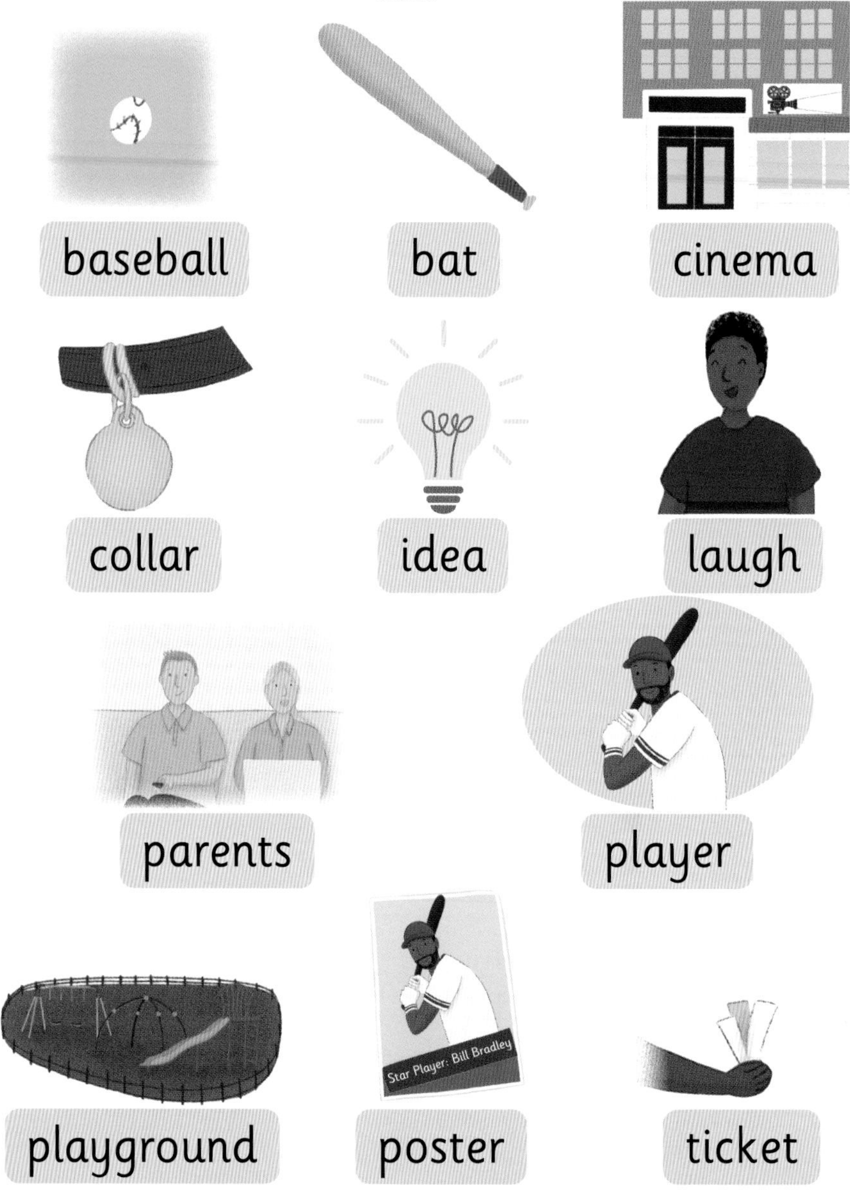

1 Look and order the story

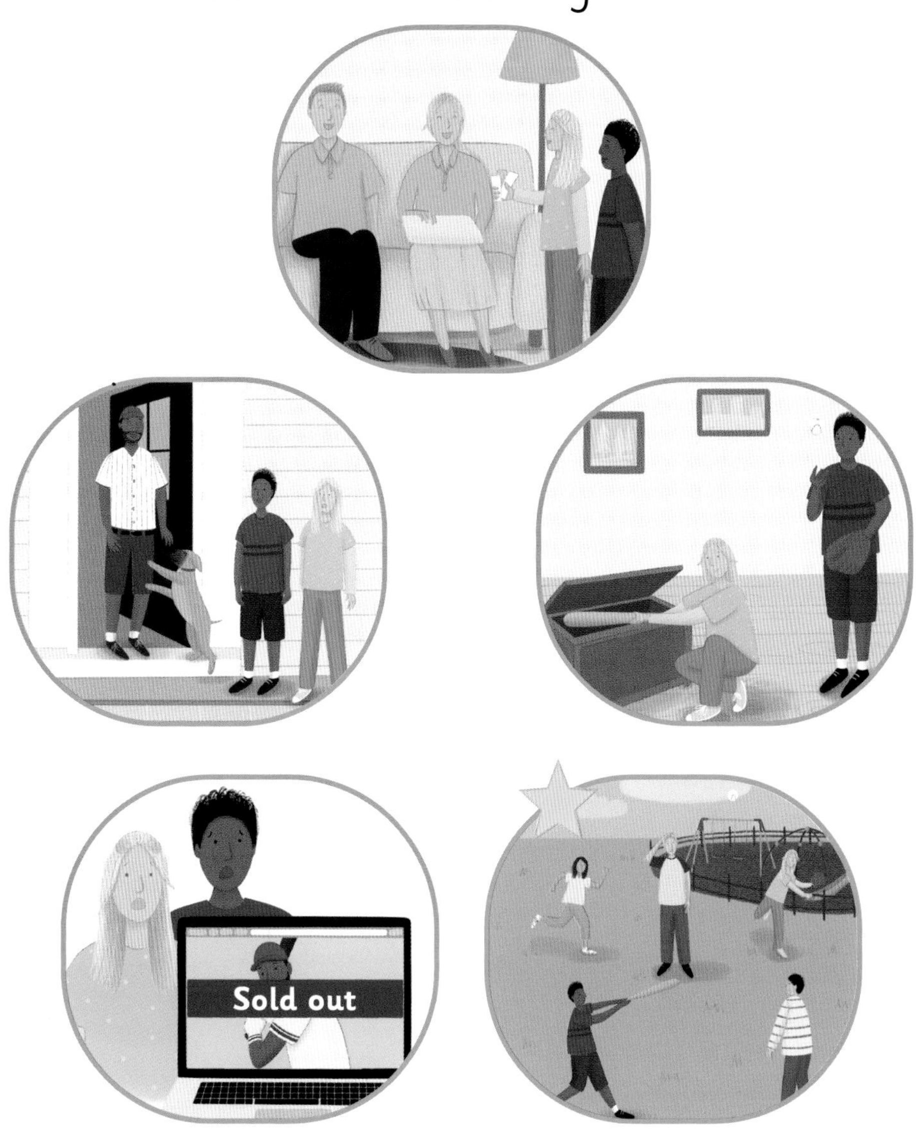

2 Listen and say  

Download a reading guide for parents and teachers at www.collins.co.uk/839706

Collins

Published by Collins
An imprint of HarperCollins*Publishers*
Westerhill Road
Bishopbriggs
Glasgow
G64 2QT

HarperCollins*Publishers*
1st Floor, Watermarque Building
Ringsend Road
Dublin 4
Ireland

William Collins' dream of knowledge for all began with the publication of his first book in 1819.

A self-educated mill worker, he not only enriched millions of lives, but also founded a flourishing publishing house. Today, staying true to this spirit, Collins books are packed with inspiration, innovation and practical expertise. They place you at the centre of a world of possibility and give you exactly what you need to explore it.

© HarperCollins*Publishers* Limited 2020

10 9 8 7 6 5 4 3 2

ISBN 978-0-00-839706-7

Collins® and COBUILD® are registered trademarks of HarperCollins*Publishers* Limited

www.collins.co.uk/elt

All rights reserved. No part of this publication may be reproduced, stored in a retrieval system, or transmitted in any form by any means, electronic, mechanical, photocopying, recording or otherwise, without the prior written permission of the Publisher or a licence permitting restricted copying in the United Kingdom issued by the Copyright Licensing Agency Ltd, 5th Floor, Shackleton House, 4 Battle Bridge Lane, London SE1 2HX.

British Library Cataloguing in Publication Data

A catalogue record for this publication is available from the British Library.

All rights reserved. No part of this book may be reproduced, stored in a retrieval system, or transmitted in any form or by any means, electronic, mechanical, photocopying, recording or otherwise, without the prior permission in writing of the Publisher. This book is sold subject to the conditions that it shall not, by way of trade or otherwise, be lent, re-sold, hired out or otherwise circulated without the Publisher's prior consent in any form of binding or cover other than that in which it is published and without a similar condition including this condition being imposed on the subsequent purchaser.

Author: Susannah Reed
Illustrator: Chloe Evans (Beehive)
Series editor: Rebecca Adlard
Commissioning editor: Zoë Clarke
Publishing manager: Lisa Todd
Product managers: Jennifer Hall and Caroline Green
In-house editor: Alma Puts Keren
Project manager: Emily Hooton
Editor: Frances Amrani
Proofreaders: Natalie Murray and Michael Lamb
Cover designer: Kevin Robbins
Typesetter: 2Hoots Publishing Services Ltd
Audio produced by id audio, London
Reading guide author: Emma Wilkinson
Production controller: Rachel Weaver
Printed and bound by: GPS Group, Slovenia

MIX
Paper from responsible sources
FSC™ C007454

This book is produced from independently certified FSC™ paper to ensure responsible forest management.

For more information visit: **www.harpercollins.co.uk/green**

Download the audio for this book and a reading guide for parents and teachers at www.collins.co.uk/839706